ZACHARY in
I'm Zachary!

For Alma

by Bertrand Gauthier
illustrations by Daniel Sylvestre

For a free color catalog describing Gareth Stevens's list of high-quality books, call 1-800-341-3569 (USA) or 1-800-461-9120 (Canada).

Library of Congress Cataloging-in-Publication Data

Gauthier, Bertrand.
   [Zunik dans Je suis Zunik. English]
   Zachary in I'm Zachary! / text by Bertrand Gauthier ; illustrated by Daniel Sylvestre.
      p.   cm. — (Just me and my dad)
   Summary: Zachary goes to kindergarten, watches television, eats pancakes, and gets mad at his father sometimes, but not for long.
   ISBN 0-8368-1007-4
   [1. Fathers and sons—Fiction.] I. Sylvestre, Daniel, ill. II. Title. III. Title: I'm Zachary! IV. Series.
PZ7.G2343Zac   1993
[E]—dc20   93-1168

This edition first published in 1993 by
Gareth Stevens Publishing
1555 North RiverCenter Drive, Suite 201
Milwaukee, Wisconsin 53212, USA

This edition first published in 1993 by Gareth Stevens, Inc. Original edition published in 1984 by Les éditions la courte échelle inc., Montréal, under the title *Zunik dans Je suis Zunik*. Text © 1984 by Bertrand Gauthier. Illustrations © 1984 by Daniel Sylvestre.

Series editor: Patricia Lantier-Sampon
Series designer: Karen Knutson

Printed in the United States of America
1 2 3 4 5 6 7 8 9 9 97 96 95 94 93

At this time, Gareth Stevens, Inc., does not use 100 percent recycled paper, although the paper used in our books does contain about 30 percent recycled fiber. This decision was made after a careful study of current recycling procedures revealed their dubious environmental benefits. We will continue to explore recycling options.

Gareth Stevens Publishing
MILWAUKEE

Every day I go to kindergarten. My friends go there, too.

We get to play, sing songs, and have fun together. Sometimes we even fight a little.

 That's David, my father, and Helen, his friend.

I like Helen, especially when she comes to get me at kindergarten with David.

I love David because he's my father and because he always takes good care of me.

Sometimes we watch television together. My father has as much fun as I do, and we always end up laughing.

7

The other day, we went to do the laundry together.

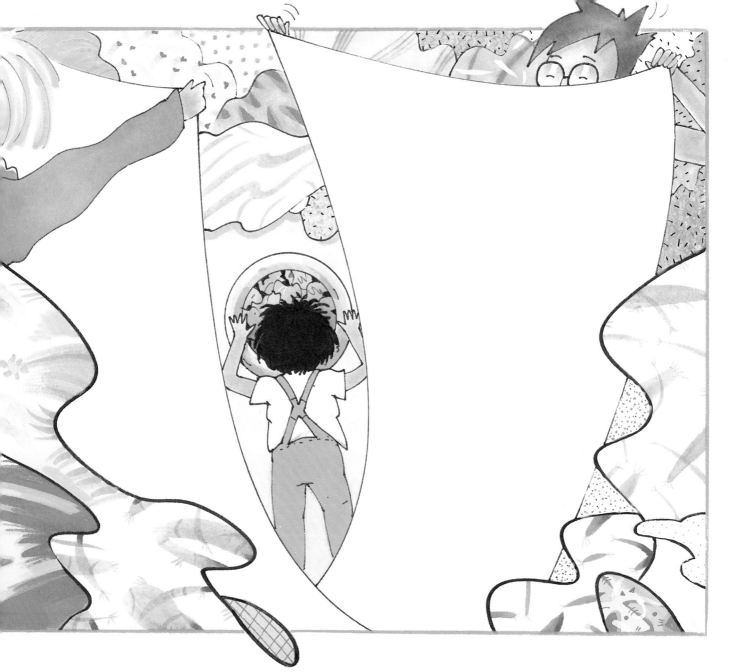

Helen came to help us fold the sheets afterward. Sheets are hard to fold, even for my father.

My father made us pancakes for lunch.
They were really good. Sometimes I wish
he would come cook for us at school.

It was a rainy Saturday afternoon. I went to the movies with Ralph and his mother.

The movie was funny. There were kids, animals, men from outer space, and a big red truck in it.

But at the end, it was very sad, and I cried.

When I got home, my father started yelling at me.

He was mad, just because I wanted to eat
chocolate chip cookies before dinner.

When I saw he was mad, I got mad, too.

 When I fell asleep, I had a strange dream.

I had wings, and I was flying above the clouds. I saw Eric's airplane that we had lost at daycare.

All of a sudden, a great big fish with wings came along. He flew up to me and gave me a sheet of paper with his picture on it.

When I woke up the next morning, I drew a picture of the wawabongbong.

Look at that!

 And I told my father about my dream.

No kidding!
Zach, we're going to send your picture to the people who write the dictionaries.